The SUPER AMAZING PRINCESS Heroes

The Gift of gift

Written by Sanjay Nambiar
Illustrated by Sedi Pak

Created for World Children's Initiative

To the supporters of World Children's Initiative,
who make this organization's amazing work possible.

Profits from this book will be shared with
World Children's Initiative,
www.worldchildrensinitiative.org.

Learn more about the fun and empowering
Super Amazing Princess Heroes universe at
www.superprincessheroes.com!

The concept for this fundraising project
was developed by Sanjay Daluvoy, M.D.

Special Thanks To:

Gift Bisikwa (the inspiration for this story);
Sanjay Daluvoy, M.D.; Kanishka Ratanayaka, M.D.;
Pratheepan Gulasekaram; Megha Kadakia;
Saurabh Kikani; Priya, Uma & Miya Nambiar;
Jeremy Cleek; Amber Ward; Nilesh Kapse; Missy,
Terrick & Myla Daluvoy; and Gina,
Mila & Miko Gulasekaram.

Copyright © 2016 by SPH Media, Inc.
All rights reserved.
Published by Umiya Publishing, Inc.

This publishing or any part thereof shall not be reproduced, stored,
copied, or transmitted (except for short quotes for the purpose of review)
in any form or by any means without written permission from the publisher.

Illustrations rendered in watercolor on birch plywood boards.
Text set in Bree Serif and Amatic SC.

For permissions information,
please contact info@superprincessheroes.com.

First Edition | 10 9 8 7 6 5 4 3 2 1
ISBN 978-0-9889050-2-3
Library of Congress Control Number 2016902478

Printed in China.

This Book Will Be Enjoyed By The Awesome Princess or prince Below:

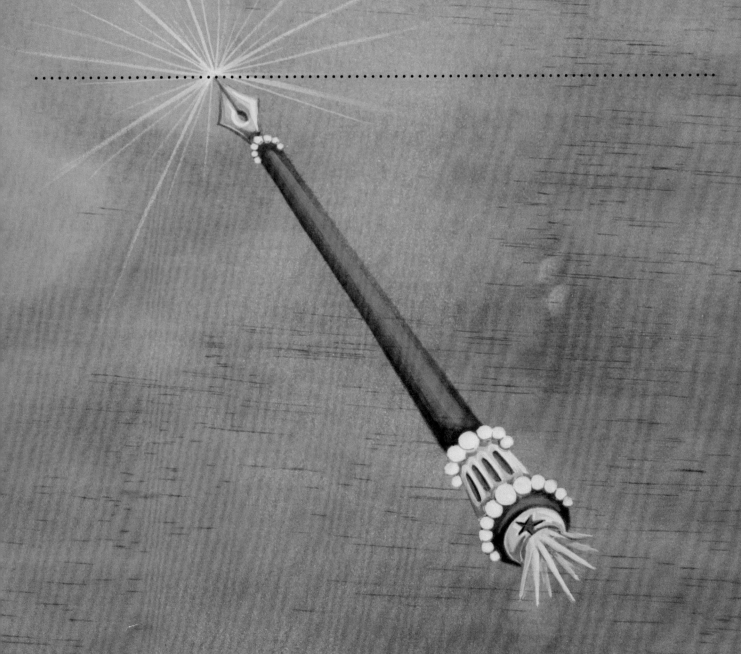

Remember the Super Amazing Princess Heroes?

Those awesome girls – Kinney, Oceana & Sammie – who transform into princesses with super powers?

Recently, they were in Uganda (a beautiful country in Africa) to help build a new school for a small village.

But only on the weekend, and only after they finished their homework, of course.

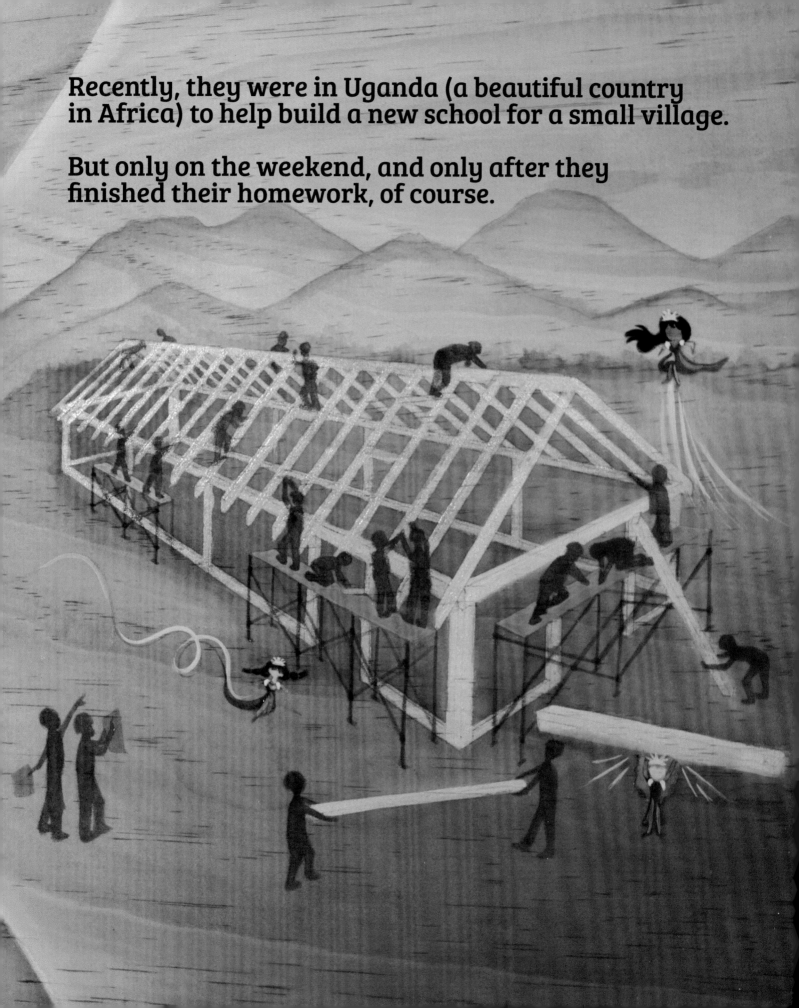

"Kinney, can you kindly procure more nails for me, please?" asked Oceana.

"Yo, no problem!" said Kinney. She used her super speed and ran to the tool shed. She was back before Oceana could blink.

"Kinney, can you grab another hammer, please?"
asked Sammie. Sammie put out her hand expecting
a hammer to be there in a second, but she felt
nothing. She looked back and still saw nothing.

A full five seconds later, Kinney finally showed up.
She was out of breath and sweating.

"Kinney! What's wrong? I've never seen you this slow,"
said Sammie.

"I don't know," said Kinney. "I don't feel good . . ."
Kinney closed her eyes and slowly fell to the ground.

When Kinney woke up,
she was at a local medical clinic.

"Girls," said Dr. K,
"Kinney is very sick. She has a hole
in her heart that's making her tired.
That's why she's running so slowly."

"IS SHE GOING TO BE OK?"

asked Sammie.

"I think so," said Dr. K. "We'll need to fly her back to America, where doctors can fix her heart."

"Is it possible to perform that procedure here?" asked Oceana.

"I'm sorry, Oceana, we can't. We just don't have the right type of hospital," said Dr. K.

The girls prepared to return home.
They said goodbye to their new friends,
especially a girl named Gift. Gift was a beautiful,
kind Ugandan girl who had become close to
Kinney, Oceana, and Sammie.

"I'LL MISS YOU!" said Gift.

The doctors in America fixed Kinney's heart and she was feeling better. As she recovered, she received a card from her friend, Gift.

After a few weeks, Kinney was
BACK TO NORMAL,
going to school and playing and enjoying life.
One day while the girls were riding bikes, Betty,
one of the Fairy Teacher Mother Superstar Queens,
visited them.

"Girls, how are you?"
asked Betty.

"Betty!" the girls yelled
together.

"We miss you! Look,
Kinney's feeling much
better!" said Sammie.

The girls gave Betty
a big hug.

"Girls, I'm sorry but I have some bad news."

The girls got quiet. Betty usually sent them to new places to help people. She never had bad news.

"Gift is sick. She actually has a hole in her heart, just like Kinney did."

Gift

"Hold up," said Kinney. "What if other kids in Uganda need the same help? It'll be hard for all of them to fly here each time."

"You're right," said Betty. "How can we help?"

"I HAVE AN IDEA," said Oceana.

"Why don't we assist Dr. K and build a hospital? With our super powers, we can complete the project very efficiently and quickly!"

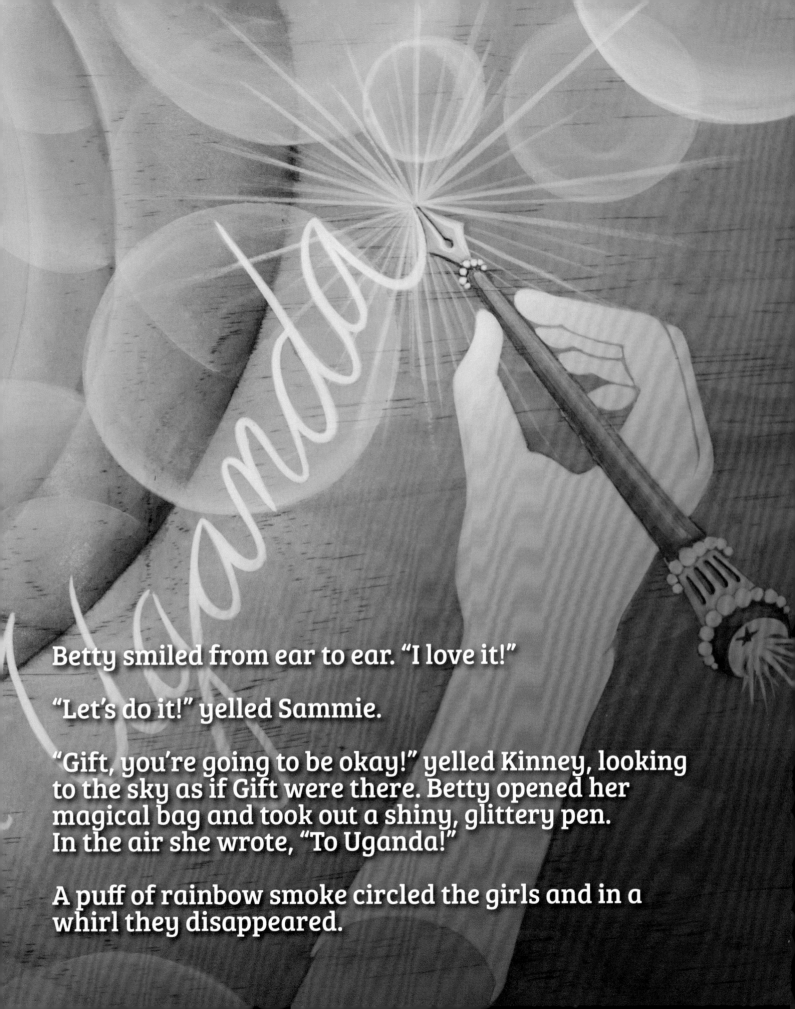

Betty smiled from ear to ear. "I love it!"

"Let's do it!" yelled Sammie.

"Gift, you're going to be okay!" yelled Kinney, looking to the sky as if Gift were there. Betty opened her magical bag and took out a shiny, glittery pen. In the air she wrote, "To Uganda!"

A puff of rainbow smoke circled the girls and in a whirl they disappeared.

Gift was in a hospital bed in Uganda.
She was over the moon to see her friends.

"What's up, Gift!" said Kinney.
"We're so sorry you're sick!"

I think I'll be fine," said Gift.
"I just hope I can go to America for help."

"Actually, you can delay those plans,"
said Oceana.

The girls worked with Dr. K and many other doctors, engineers, builders, and business people. Using their super speed, incredible strength, and flying powers, they helped build a beautiful hospital.

HOSPITAL

WORLD CHILDREN'S INITIATIVE | LINE 1

SPH
CONSTRUCTION, INC

CHILDREN BORN WITH HEART PROBLEMS IN UGANDA

10,000 EVERY YEAR

And guess what happened next?

GIFT'S HEART SURGERY WAS SUCCESSFUL!

A few weeks later, Gift was playing at home when the girls visited her.

"Gift, how are you?" asked Sammie.

"I feel great! Thank you so much for everything you girls did!"

"Actually, thank you, Gift," said Kinney. "You're such an awesome friend. You helped us build that school, and when I got sick, you were there for me."

SUDDENLY,
a cloud of purple smoke rose from the corner of the room.

From it appeared Betty! "Who is that?" asked Gift.

"That's Betty, our Fairy Teacher Mother Superstar Queen," said Oceana.

"Hi, Betty!" said the girls together.

"Gift," said Betty,
"you are a truly special girl. You're a great friend.
You're brave and smart, and you're humble."

"Thank you so much, Ms. Betty," said Gift.

"Oh, you can just call me Betty.
Anyway, I have a little present for you."

Betty was holding a special bag.
It was the same bag that the Super Amazing Princess Heroes
found in the forest once. Betty pulled out a beautiful,

SHIMMERING TIARA

with a yellow jewel in the middle.

"Go ahead, try it on," said Betty.

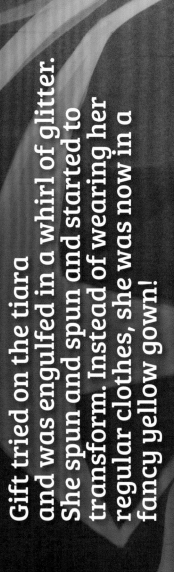

Gift tried on the tiara and was engulfed in a whirl of glitter. She spun and spun and started to transform. Instead of wearing her regular clothes, she was now in a fancy yellow gown!

"Congratulations, Gift!" said Betty.

"YOU ARE NOW A SUPER AMAZING PRINCESS HERO!"

You have the power of healing. You can help kids get better faster, play harder, and live longer."

"Thank you, thank you, thank you!" said Gift.

"We can't wait for you to meet the other Super Amazing Princess Heroes," said Sammie.

"Wait, there are more?!" said Gift.

Betty smiled at Gift.

Indeed, there are many more Super Amazing Princess Heroes, and they're ready to help change the world.

BE YOU. BE POWERFUL.
BE A SUPER AMAZING PRINCESS HERO!

About WCI

World Children's Initiative ("WCI") is a non-profit organization dedicated to improving and rebuilding the healthcare and educational infrastructure for children in developing areas both in the U.S. and worldwide.

In the fall of 2010, WCI flew Gift, a 5-year-old Ugandan girl, and her mother to Washington, D.C. to repair a hole in her heart. Gift's recovery has been remarkable, and to her mom's delight, she is now enjoying an active and happy childhood. After Gift's successful surgery, WCI helped develop a Children's Heart Program at Mulago Hospital in Uganda. By training doctors in Uganda, helping build a catheterization lab, and developing a supply chain, WCI has created a long-lasting solution for Ugandan children to get the cardiac care they need and in their home country.

WCI's motto:
Helping Children Live Longer and Play Harder.